Contents

1	The Countdown Crew	1
2	The Pearl of One Thousand Blessings	5
3	Lord Percy's Travel Trunk	17
4	Gotcha!	22
5	Yeti Fur	27
6	"Great Scott, McNab!"	40
7	Molly Spills the Beans	47
8	Joe Gets a Text	53
9	Show-down at Tarzan Towers	58

Ways to Trap a Yeti

by

Annie Dalton

Illustrated by Mike Phillips

To Sophie and Izzie

First published in 2010 in Great Britain by
Barrington Stoke Ltd
18 Walker St, Edinburgh, EH3 7LP

www.barringtonstoke.co.uk

Reprinted 2012

ISBN: 978-1-84299-761-1

Printed in China by Leo

Chapter 1
The Countdown Crew

Every morning Joe Kelly woke with his heart thumping. *Will it be today? Will they get me today?*

Last week the gang got Alfie, one of Joe's mates. It was just a matter of time before they got Joe.

Joe didn't tell anyone his worries. Gramps had enough on. Gran was in hospital and he had to run the junk shop on his own. He didn't tell his sister, Molly, because she was only six and a half. Joe thought that was too young to worry about gangs.

Then one afternoon he walked in from school and she almost bit his head off!

"You have to wear your hood *up*, stupid! Then the Countdown Crew can't get your picture!"

Joe was shocked. "How did you know about that?"

She made a face at him. "Everyone knows."

"Don't tell Gramps, OK!" he hissed.

"She already told me," Gramps shouted from the kitchen. He was washing grapes for Gran.

"Thanks, Moll," Joe muttered.

Gramps turned off the tap. "I just don't understand why bullies need to take a photo of you."

"To blackmail you, Gramps," Joe said. "You have to give them something."

"If you don't give them what they want, they send a really embarrassing picture all round the school," Molly told him.

"Do they want money?" asked Gramps.

"Or your iPod or your new trainers," Joe said.

Gramps looked shocked. "Who are these kids?"

Joe didn't want to say. What was the point? Everyone knew who they were but no one did anything.

"Stand up to them, Joe, that's what I say. Bullies are all cowards really," Gramps said.

He didn't understand, Joe thought. The Countdown Crew didn't just smack you around and steal your stuff. They put your face on the internet. By the time they'd finished you were just a big joke.

What would they do when it was Joe's turn? Make him cry like a girl, or bark like a dog? Tie him to a lamp post and leave him there all night?

Molly was twisting her Barbie's head round and round on its neck. "If I get hold of those bullies I'll – OUF! – like this!" And she pulled its head right off.

"That'd teach them!" Gramps laughed. "Come on, kids, let's go and cheer up your gran."

Chapter 2

The Pearl of One Thousand Blessings

Even in hospital Gran was in charge.

"I hope Gramps is looking after you. Is he giving you proper food?" she said with a grin. "Five helpings of fruit and veg a day?"

"Do oven chips count?" Joe asked.

Gramps looked hurt. "I give you frozen peas too!"

"Joe's just teasing," said Gran.

"Will they let you out in time for Christmas, Gran?" asked Molly.

"Maybe! I'm crossing my fingers!"

Gran turned to Gramps. "You haven't forgotten that big sale at Pimm Hall? This weekend, isn't it?"

He shook his head. "No – the sale's tomorrow. I can't go. It's too far away and I can't leave the kids that long."

Joe had heard Gramps talk about Pimm Hall before. "Didn't your grandpa used to work there?"

Gramps nodded. "But it was my great grandpa Kelly, not my gramps! He was the butler there. Now Pimm Hall is being turned into a hotel so everything's got to be sold off."

"Your gramps has always wanted to solve an old mystery. He wants to find out what really happened to Lord Percy," said Gran.

"What mystery?" asked Molly.

At the same moment Joe said, "Who was Lord Percy?"

"Tell them, Stan," said Gran.

Gramps took off his glasses and put on his best story-telling voice. "We're talking about a long time ago. Over a hundred years ago, Queen Victoria had died and Edward was our king."

"Were there cars?" asked Molly.

Gramps nodded. "Lord Percy had one of the first motor cars in Norfolk. Drove it like a madman. He was always wild, even as a boy."

"Did he bite?" asked Molly at once.

Gramps laughed. "Don't know about that but he always hated to be indoors. His brothers grew up and got proper jobs, married nice wives. But Percy longed for adventure."

Gramps was an excellent story-teller. Even the lady in the next bed was listening in!

Gramps popped one of Gran's grapes in his mouth and went on with his story. "Lord Percy's father told him he had to settle down and earn some money. But Lord Percy didn't care! He was off to see the world! And that's what he did. Off he went, getting himself into all kinds of trouble. As years went by Lord Percy found ways to make money from his travels. He tracked down weird bits and pieces to sell when he got home."

"Like what?" asked Molly.

"Precious statues, jewels, exotic animals, anything he could sell for a profit," Gramps said.

"Did he pay for them?" Joe asked but he'd already guessed the answer.

Gramps looked embarrassed. "Englishmen thought the world was all theirs for the taking in those days. They never paid for anything if they could help it."

Like the Countdown Crew, thought Joe.

"One night Lord Percy was in a bar in the Far East. He heard some men talking about a pearl that brought good luck to anyone who owned it. The locals called it the Pearl of One Thousand Blessings. The men said it was hidden in a cave somewhere in Tibet. For hundreds of years different explorers had tried to find this pearl but they'd all vanished. No one knew how or where."

Molly gave a shiver. "I don't like the sound of this."

Gramps put an arm around her. "Lord Percy made up his mind to get his hands on the pearl. He needed some cash first so he came back to England. My great grandpa said he'd never seen Lord Percy so excited. 'I'm going to make my fortune, Kelly, and when I do, I'll buy you a fat cigar!' Lord Percy told him. That was the last time my great gramps saw Lord Percy or his servant, McNab."

"I knew it was going to get scary," Molly said in a small voice.

"You big baby," said Joe.

Gramps went on with his story. "Months passed. One day a friend of Lord Percy's received a letter from him. Lord Percy was in Tibet and he had a problem. The local people wouldn't help him look for the pearl. They said the pearl was protected by a dangerous yeti. They told Lord Percy to go home and forget the whole idea."

"What do yetis look like?" Molly asked in the same little voice.

Joe laughed. "Like giant hair balls in snow-shoes! They don't exist, don't worry."

Gramps shook his head. "Lord Percy thought different. This news just made him want the pearl even more. He decided to bag the pearl AND the yeti."

Joe gave a snigger. "What a crackpot! What was he going to do with a yeti?"

Molly looked at him as if he was stupid. "Sell it to a zoo of course! Don't you know anything, Joe?"

Gramps pinched another grape.

"Lord Percy waited and waited but there was no news of the pearl or the yeti. He was ready to give up. Then he had a stroke of luck. A young hunter said he'd seen yeti foot-prints on a nearby mountain. He said he'd help Lord Percy follow the trail. Maybe it would lead them to the cave where the pearl was hidden. In his letter, Lord Percy promised his friend a fat cigar when he'd made his fortune. But the friend never got his cigar."

Molly looked sad. "Because Lord Percy never came back. What happened to him, Gramps?"

"No one really knows. We know that Lord Percy and the others set off to follow the yeti's trail into the mountains. Then something odd happened. The local people said there wasn't a cloud to be seen, then a snow storm suddenly swept down out of nowhere. They said the snow didn't fall like normal snow. It was falling just on one side of the mountain."

"Where Lord Percy was," breathed Molly.

Gramps nodded. "That's right. Days later the hunter stumbled back into the village. He was alone. He said Lord Percy and McNab, his servant, had been taken by the yeti. Neither of them was heard of again."

Gran smiled at the children. "Your gramps always dreamed of finding a letter or an old diary that might help explain what really happened."

Molly gasped. "We must all go to the sale tomorrow, Gramps! We'll help you look for clues!"

Gran looked at Gramps. "It wouldn't hurt to take a day off school just this once."

"Just don't bring back a yeti!" called the lady in the next bed.

Suddenly everyone was laughing, even Joe. For the first time in weeks he let himself relax. He was getting a day off! A whole day without worrying about the Countdown Crew!

Chapter 3
Lord Percy's Travel Trunk

It was still dark when they set off in Gramps' old van. Molly went back to sleep. She didn't wake up till Gramps' car turned into the long road through the park around Pimm Hall. Rows of cars were parked outside.

"The dealers are here already," said Gramps.

"Quick, everyone, before they find all the clues!" Molly shouted. She started running towards the house.

Inside the house it was mad. Joe thought it would be a proper sale – an auction with people shouting out bids. But it was more like a massive indoor car boot sale with old furniture and junk stacked up everywhere. The children squeezed between rails full of smelly old clothes.

Joe spent ages hunting through boxes of books but he didn't find anything that looked like a diary.

They heard a sudden screech from Molly. "You've got to see this!"

They found her looking longingly at an old doll's house.

"You don't like dolls, Moll. You just like pulling them apart," Joe told her.

Molly folded her arms. "But it's a real house with fireplaces and everything."

"It's a good buy, Joe," Gramps said. "It's a perfect replica of Pimm Hall. If Molly doesn't play with it, we can put it on eBay."

Molly hugged him round his knees. "Thank you, Gramps!"

Her happy mood didn't last. After another hour she started moaning. "I'm really hot and my head hurts. I think I'm poorly."

Gramps said they'd better go home.

Molly burst into tears. "But I wanted to find a clue!"

Gramps picked her up and Joe followed them through the crowd. Suddenly he spotted some paintings heaped on top of an old box. Then he took a second look at the box.

"Gramps! You'll want to see this!"

They all stared down at the old box. It was a trunk – a sort of huge suitcase people had long ago. An old luggage label was still tied to the handle. The ink had blurred so they couldn't read the name.

"How much is the old trunk?" Gramps asked the lady.

She looked surprised. "That? You can have it for a tenner."

In the car park Molly jumped up and down. "Open it, Gramps! Let's see if it's Lord Percy's."

But the trunk had a rusty lock – and no key.

"We'll saw through the lock when we get home," Gramps told them.

Joe had stopped listening. A text had just popped up on his phone: **u can run but you cant hide**.

The Countdown Crew were coming to get him.

Chapter 4
Gotcha!

They didn't open the trunk when they got home. Molly really had caught a bug and had to be put to bed.

But Joe couldn't sleep. The next day he looked so pale Gramps said maybe he should stay home too. He shook his head. Germs couldn't save him. Nothing could.

They'll get me on the way home, Joe thought. That's when the Countdown Crew liked to strike.

When he walked out of school it was starting to snow. His mates walked with him as far as Cost Cutter. Gramps had texted him to buy eggs. Friday night was egg and chips night. His mates didn't fancy waiting around for him in the cold. They hurried off without him.

Joe felt sick. *They're watching*, he thought. Now he was alone the gang would make their move.

In the supermarket they were playing carols. Joe paid at the check-out then walked back into the falling snow. He was so scared he couldn't remember how to breathe. But there was no one waiting. Joe went dizzy with relief.

"Gotcha!"

Someone grabbed him. They'd been hiding behind the wheelie bins.

The kids crowded around Joe.

One went through Joe's pockets. "No cash and his phone is rubbish!" he sneered.

The leader gave Joe a slow grin. "That's not very clever, Joe. Didn't anyone tell you? Nobody messes with the Countdown Crew. Tell him, boys!"

It was like a signal. The gang started to chant their famous countdown. "Ten, nine, eight!"

One kid pulled up Joe's jacket. "Seven, six!"

Another tugged at Joe's trousers and sniggered.

"Five, four, three, two!"

Joe felt a rush of freezing cold air and made a mad grab at his trousers. Too late. They went down round his trainers.

"ONE!"

SPLOSH!

Six eggs smashed on to the pavement.

Flash! One of the kids snapped a picture of Joe with his mobile. They raced away howling with laughter. They'd got their picture. Joe in his boxers in a puddle of broken eggs.

Chapter 5
Yeti Fur

Joe's shoes and socks made sloshing sounds as he ran. Everything smelled of egg. By the time he got home to Gramps' shop, his eggy clothes felt totally frozen.

He let himself in the side door. Molly and Gramps were in the shop. Gramps called, "Joe, you're just in time! We're going to open the trunk."

Joe didn't care. He didn't want to talk to anyone ever again. He sloshed across the hall making eggy footprints.

Molly ran out to meet him. "Where've you been?"

"They got me," Joe told her and ran upstairs.

No one wanted to open the trunk after that.

Gramps made Joe take off his eggy things and ran him a hot bath. There were no eggs for tea so he phoned out for a pizza.

Molly went to sit beside Joe. "What are you going to do?"

Joe didn't have a choice. "I'll have to give them my birthday money."

"But you really wanted to buy that new game," Molly said.

Joe turned on the TV loud. “I don’t want to talk about it.”

Molly threw the remote across the room then burst into tears.

Joe woke in the middle of the night. He heard Molly creeping downstairs. He found her kneeling beside Lord Percy’s travel trunk.

“I can’t make this work!” Molly said softly. She was trying to saw through the lock with Gramps’ hacksaw.

"At two in the morning?" Joe hissed. "Are you mad? Plus you'll saw off your fingers!"

His sister's eyes were bright. "Joe, what if Lord Percy found the pearl before he was got by the yeti? What if he gave it to the hunter and he put it in the trunk?"

"That's a lot of what-ifs," Joe said.

Molly grabbed his hand. "The pearl is magic, Joe! We could blast the Countdown Crew into outer space forever!"

"I bet the trunk's empty," said Joe. "I bet Lord Percy's family took everything out long ago."

But there was no point talking to his sister in this mood. Joe had to help her.

He went to find Gramps' bolt cutters and broke the lock. "Just don't get your hopes up, OK?" he told Molly.

He took a deep breath and lifted the lid. A weird smell rushed out, sweet, musty, spicy. *The trunk wasn't empty.*

Suddenly Joe was as excited as Molly. They started lifting things out – a compass, an old fashioned sun helmet, a chess set, a pack of playing cards.

"Lord Percy wore huge pants," Molly giggled. She held up a pair of long johns.

Joe spotted a book hidden under the long johns. "Does that look like a diary to you?"

A street lamp outside gave just enough light to read by.

Joe turned to the first page and Molly gave a squeak. "Joe, it is his, look!"

"This book belongs to Lord Percy Alfred Pimm," Joe read.

The book was more like a notebook than a diary. It was full of jottings and drawings. On one page Lord Percy had glued in a thick lock of strange white hair.

"What is that?" Molly said.

Joe gave a shrug. "His girlfriend's?"

Molly shook her head. "That's yeti fur, Joe."

"How many times, Moll? Yetis don't exist!"

"What's that then?" Molly pointed to the blurred photo glued next to the lock of hair.

"Haven't got a clue!" Joe thought it looked like a cross between a giant tree and a walking cloud.

"It's the yeti! You just won't admit it!" Molly insisted.

"You're dreaming," Joe told her.

"Lord Percy didn't think it was a dream, look!" Molly said.

At the top of the next page Lord Percy had written:

Ways to catch a Yeti ...

There were pages of drawings of strange yeti-catching devices – traps, pits, nets. Lord Percy had written in the margins too – things like *Do yetis have a sweet tooth? Could use honey as bait.*

"Totally bonkers," Joe said to himself.

Molly had gone back to the trunk. "I'm looking for the pearl so I can show Gramps when ... " She gave a squeak.

Joe went to see what she'd found.

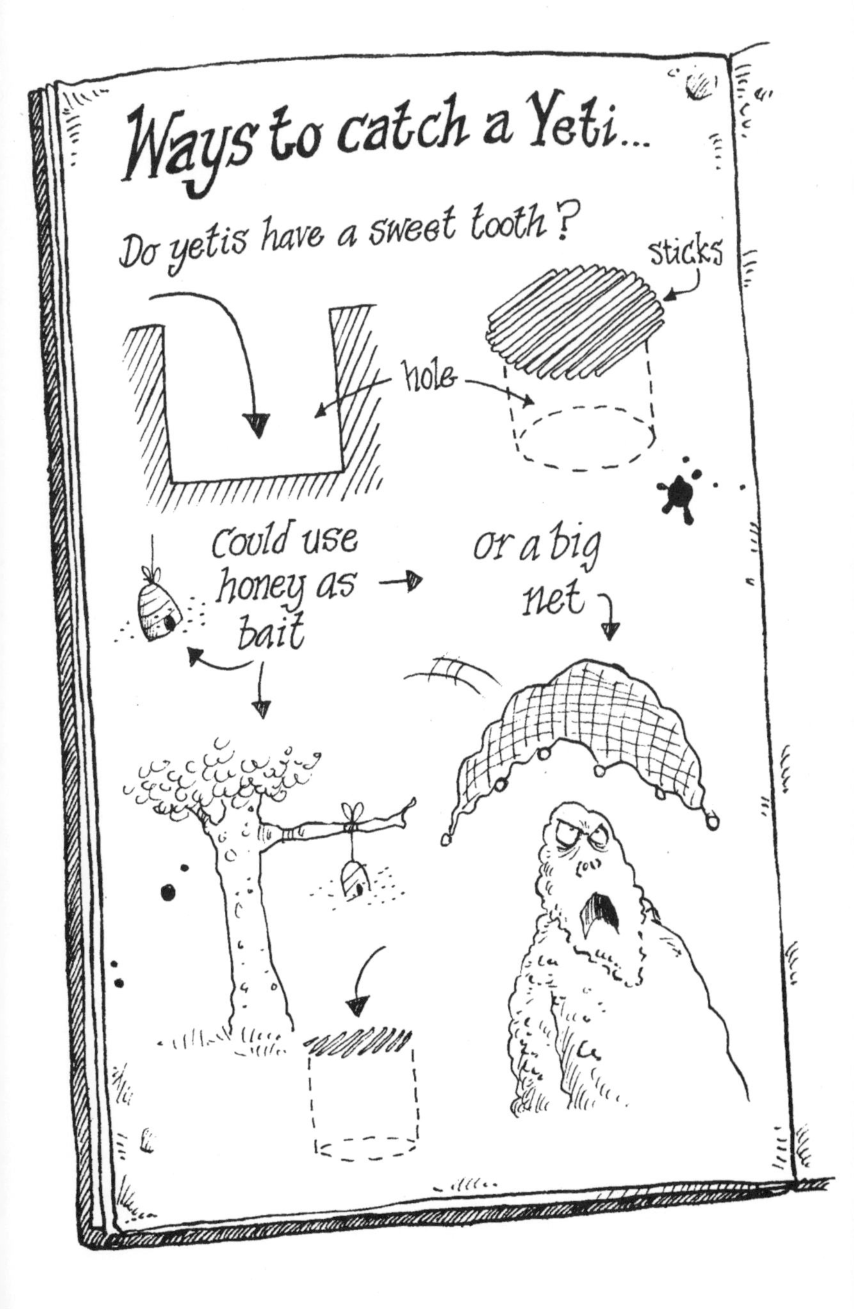
Ways to catch a Yeti...
Do yetis have a sweet tooth?
sticks
hole
Could use honey as bait
or a big net

At the bottom of the trunk was a wooden box. Odd-looking patterns were carved into the wood.

Molly's eyes were huge. "Joe, it's the pearl! I can feel the magic! It's like, really cold and buzzy!"

Joe touched the box. It felt like touching the ice-cube tray in the freezer. Joe didn't believe in magic but this box gave him serious goosebumps.

He felt around the box for a catch.

"How are you meant to open it?" he muttered.

He fetched a screw-driver and tried to force the lid.

"You're doing it all wrong, Joe," Molly moaned.

"You do it then!" he snapped.

She burst into tears. "But I'm too little and I'm not even very well!"

It had been a long day and Joe finally lost it.

He jabbed his finger at the box. "Just open up, OK! Before I murder my little sister!"

"Woo!" Molly grabbed at Joe's arm.

Slowly, without a sound, the box was opening all by itself!

When she saw inside, Molly's eyes got even bigger.

"Joe, look! Fairies!" she said.

He pulled her away. "They're not fairies. They've got guns."

Chapter 6
"Great Scott, McNab!"

The tiny men stared at them in shock.

"They're just nippers, milord," one whispered.

"Sorry, old chap. Bit too quick on the draw there," said the other little man in a posh voice. Both men looked like old-fashioned explorers. They had baggy trousers and walking boots. The posh little man had a big sandy moustache that curled up at the corners.

They're very chirpy for people who've been locked inside a box, Joe thought.

The tiny men quickly put down their guns.

The little man with the curly moustache looked embarrassed. "Frightfully sorry about that!" he said. "A chap gets a bit trigger happy when he's been shut in a box for ... what year is this?"

Molly told him.

He looked shocked. "Great Scott, McNab! That's more than a hundred years! No wonder you're a bit peckish!"

Molly clapped her hands. "He said 'McNab'! Remember, Joe? Lord Percy's servant was called Spoons McNab!"

The posh little man gave them a polite bow. "Lord Percy Pimm at your service! And this is indeed my trusty manservant, McNab!" He turned to his friend. "It seems you're famous, McNab!" he added with a grin.

He looked up at Joe. "Would you mind giving us a hand out, old bean? Never could stand small spaces."

Joe helped him out. He felt as if he was in a dream. Then he lifted McNab out of the box and stood him carefully beside Lord Percy. Without thinking, he'd put them next to some old fashioned perfume bottles from Gramps' shop. The tallest bottle was about six cm high and that was still a bit taller than Lord Percy.

This has to be a dream, he thought.

McNab winked at him. “What’s your name, nipper?”

“I’m Joe Kelly. This is my sister Molly.” Joe felt daft talking to someone who was only six cm tall.

Molly didn’t see a problem. She started chatting right away.

“Did you know they’re turning your house into a hotel, Lord Percy? They had a massive sale. That’s where Joe found your trunk.”

“Turning it into a hotel? Are you sure?” Lord Percy had to look away and blink a few times. He pulled himself together. “Have to expect a few changes, eh what, McNab?”

“We’ve got our health, milord, that’s the main thing,” McNab said.

Lord Percy slapped him on the back. "An excellent man in a tight spot, McNab! Couldn't even get my silly boots off without McNab!"

Molly was shocked. "You can't take off your own boots! What kind of grown up are you?" she asked.

"The kind who robs other people's treasures, and hunts down rare animals," said Joe.

"I've mended my ways since then, dear boy," Lord Percy said with a grin. "Look, sorry to be a bore, but McNab's belly is making the most frightful noise. Don't suppose you could find him a small snack?"

Molly nodded. "There's some pizza. It's cold but we can put it in the microwave. Joe didn't want his. He was too upset ..."

"Shut UP," Joe told her.

But Molly wasn't interested in Joe. "Aren't you hungry, Lord Percy?" she asked in a worried voice. "You've been in that box a REALLY long time."

Lord Percy's stomach give a long noisy gurgle. He coughed to cover the sound. "Just a bite then, if you really insist. Just to keep McNab company!"

Chapter 7
Molly Spills the Beans

In the end, Lord Percy guzzled down loads of pizza. Then he wanted a bath.

Joe was longing to get back to bed but he boiled a kettle and filled tiny doll's house jugs with hot water. McNab lugged them up the stairs of the doll's house, whistling.

Molly shut the doll's house up so Lord Percy could have his bath in private.

Using the doll's house was her idea. "It's like a teeny-weeny Pimm Hall. They'll feel really at home," she told Joe happily.

At last Lord Percy was ready. He stood in his doll's house room in his dressing gown, looking pink and smelling of Gran's best bath oil. "I'm a new man. I'll be needing a shave tomorrow, McNab."

Lord Percy was starting to get right up Joe's nose. You'd think a hundred years in a box would knock all the swank out of him but he was still lording it around.

"I think it's time you told us how you got inside that box," Joe said in his coldest voice.

"I could tell you that," said Molly to his surprise.

She gave Lord Percy a big smile. "It was the yeti, wasn't it? He didn't want you to steal the pearl, and he didn't want to be sent to a zoo."

Lord Percy gave a deep sigh. "I'm afraid you're right."

He told them what Molly had guessed. The yeti was not a hairy monster out of a cartoon. He was old and wise with special magical powers.

The giant yeti had suddenly loomed out of the snow storm. He was so tall he towered over the humans. He shrank Lord Percy and his servant, McNab until they exactly fitted inside his magic box. Using a special yeti spell, he locked them in.

"But it was just until you learned your lesson," Molly said. "You're truly sorry about all that bad stuff you did, or the yeti wouldn't have let you out," said Molly.

Lord Percy was impressed. "You really are an extremely clever child," he said.

He tried to hide a yawn. "Forgive me. This has all been rather tiring."

"Your bed is made up with clean sheets, milord, if you wish to retire," said McNab.

"I believe I will grab a little spot of shut-eye," yawned Lord Percy.

As he started up the stairs, he turned to Joe. "I'd rather you didn't tell your grandparents about us, old bean. Not until we've done what we came to do. Don't want to find ourselves in a peep show on Brighton Pier! 'The Two Tiny Men'!"

"What have you come to do?" asked Joe.

But no one heard.

"They'd put you on YouTube now," said Molly.

Lord Percy looked amazed. "YouTube, microwaves. The future is a strange and wonderful country, McNab."

"Indeed, milord," said McNab.

"What have you come to do?" Joe asked, this time in a louder voice.

Lord Percy gave him a warm smile. “Send those bullies away with their tails between their legs, of course!”

Joe felt himself turning red. “How do you know about them?”

“Your sister rather spilled the beans, old chum,” said Lord Percy.

“While you were boiling the kettle for milord’s bath,” McNab went on.

“And did you all have a good laugh?” Joe snapped.

Molly looked upset. “You don’t get it. Lord Percy and Spoons McNab want to help you. Tell him, Spoons!”

McNab sounded as calm as always. “The yeti shut us in the box until someone needed us to do them a good deed. I reckon you’re that someone, Joe!”

Chapter 8
Joe Gets a Text

Lord Percy slept all next day.

After lunch, Joe peeped in the doll's house and saw him. He was still asleep and snoring softly in the four poster bed.

McNab was downstairs polishing Lord Percy's boots. "His lordship asked not to be disturbed," he told Joe firmly.

"Great," said Joe. After Monday he'd be dead and Lord Percy didn't want to be disturbed!

He stormed off to find his Xbox.

"Spoons is giving the doll's house a really good spring clean," Molly whispered at lunch-time.

Spoons McNab had been stuck in the box with Lord Percy for more than a hundred years. Yet Lord Percy got to snooze the day away and McNab was doing all the work. It made Joe mad.

After tea he'd had enough. He marched into his sister's room in the mood to pick a fight.

Molly gave him a big smile. "Spoons was just telling me about his bad boy days in Peckham."

McNab was sitting in the doll's house kitchen. He was sewing a button on Lord Percy's shirt. He bit off a piece of cotton. "But then I met his lordship and changed my ways. Who knows where I'd be without Lord Percy."

"You wouldn't have got stuck in a box for one thing!" Joe pointed out.

"Just one of life's little set-backs," McNab said.

Molly started to giggle. "Do people call you Spoons McNab because you used to nab spoons?"

He grinned at her. "Actually, that's not why. This is why they call me Spoons!"

McNab pulled four tiny spoons out of the kitchen dresser. He started smacking them up and down his arms and legs. The flying spoons sounded exactly like Spanish castanets.

Lord Percy came in still wearing his dressing gown. “Bit of a party, what?” He grabbed more spoons and joined in McNab’s very rude East End song.

Molly laughed so hard she cried. “I want them to live in my doll’s house forever!” she told Joe.

Joe felt his phone start to buzz. He had a photo text.

The photo was of Joe. A Joe with no trousers in a puddle of broken eggs. The text said: **next time it wont just be ur eggs we break**.

Chapter 9
Show-down at Tarzan Towers

"I was stupid to listen to you! How can you help me? I've seen bigger nits than you!" Joe shouted at Lord Percy.

"You're upset, old bean," Lord Percy said.

"Because my life is OVER!" Joe yelled.

"It isn't over yet, nipper. Not by a long chalk. His lordship is working on a plan," said McNab.

"In his SLEEP!!" Joe shouted back. He was so mad he wanted to jump up and down.

"His lordship will see you right," McNab said firmly.

Lord Percy was thinking. "Joe, I want you to send a message back to those thugs. But this time we won't take any chances."

He turned to Molly. "Do you know anywhere with a good look-out? Something high you could climb up?"

"Tarzan Towers!" she said at once.

"I'm not meeting the gang at the adventure playground. No way!" said Joe.

Lord Percy just ignored him. "Is there a tower at Tarzan Towers?" he asked.

Molly nodded. "A HUGE one with a brilliant slide."

Lord Percy thought for a moment. "Joe, send a return message to the gang. Tell them you'll be at Tarzan Towers at 3pm tomorrow with the money."

Molly shook her head. "We always visit Gran at three."

"Can't let your gran down," McNab agreed.

"2pm then," said Lord Percy.

Joe scowled. "And what will you be doing? Using your killer kung fu on them, I suppose?"

Lord Percy laughed. "Much better than kung fu, dear boy. Don't you worry about a thing."

Easy for him to say. It wasn't Lord Percy's underwear that was going on show, Joe thought.

Molly was pink with excitement. "I can't wait to see you beat the gang, Joe!"

"You've got a long wait then because you're not coming," said Joe.

"Sorry, old chum, but we need Molly up in the tower," Lord Percy said in a firm voice.

Joe wasn't having it. "This is my little sister we're talking about and she stays home."

Lord Percy shook his head. "It won't work without her."

Joe stared at him. "Are you saying you have a real plan?"

"Didn't I say his lordship will see you right?" McNab said with a grin.

Lord Percy had been looking over at Molly's TV, which she'd left on mute. Tiger cubs padded across the screen.

"So that's what a YouTube looks like," Lord Percy said.

Molly giggled. "No, that's just my TV."

He looked puzzled. "It's showing us tigers now, but before that it was polar bears."

Molly pulled a sad face. "Probably a film about animals that are getting extinct."

Lord Percy looked shocked. "Tigers are extinct in your time?"

"Most things are nearly extinct now, aren't they, Joe?"

Like me, thought Joe.

Late on Sunday morning a text came back from the gang: **ok but dont try anything**.

"Bring your wallet but empty it first," said Lord Percy.

"Joe's wallet is always empty," Molly said with a sigh.

At fifteen minutes to two, Joe told Gramps that he and Molly had to go out to buy Gran a Christmas present.

"I'll come too. We'll visit your gran on the way home," Gramps said at once.

"You can't!" Molly said before Joe could open his mouth.

Gramps looked surprised. "Why not?"

Molly tapped her nose. "Joe doesn't want me to say."

"Oh, I see!" Gramps said with a grin.

He thought they were buying his present too.

"Liar, liar, pants on fire," Joe whispered as they hurried out.

"I wasn't lying! You didn't want me to tell Gramps you're having a show-down at Tarzan Towers!"

Lord Percy was in Joe's top pocket. Molly let McNab ride in the front of her shoulder bag so he could see out. Lord Percy was amazed by the traffic. He wanted Joe to tell him the models of all the cars. But McNab wasn't impressed. "London don't look right without the horses."

At Tarzan Towers, kids in woolly hats and scarves were playing in the slush. They seemed as if they didn't have a worry in the world, Joe thought.

Lord Percy looked round the playground. He grinned. "This is perfect. Molly, get up the tower as fast as you can. Joe, give her your phone!"

The Countdown Crew would be arriving any minute to collect their cash and Joe was being bossed about by a posh little man who ate off dolly plates. Lord Percy had totally taken charge and Joe was just letting him.

"I'm the one that's going to get creamed. Could you just tell me what's going on?" Joe was suddenly mad enough to spit.

Molly was speeding up the ladder to the tower. "We can't because you wouldn't believe us!" she shouted.

That did it! Joe went to grab Lord Percy by his jacket. "You told Molly and you didn't tell me!" Next minute he heard his sister yell down from the tower.

"I can see them! They're coming through the gates!"

Joe felt sick. The Countdown Crew came into the playground as if they owned the place.

The other kids quickly got out of the way.

Joe and the gang stared at each other across the playground. Joe could feel his knees shaking.

"Did you bring our cash?" the leader wanted to know.

"Say 'yes'," whispered Lord Percy.

"I said I would, didn't I?" yelled Joe.

"You know that plan everyone else knows about? Now would be a really good time to share!" he hissed at Lord Percy.

Lord Percy gave a soft chuckle. "He'll be here any minute. Didn't you notice it's started snowing?"

Lord Percy was right. It was suddenly snowing heavily, a strange swirly kind of snow that fell in only one corner of the playground.

The gang didn't care about the weather. They went on walking towards Joe.

"Show us the money if you've got it?" one snarled.

"Show them," whispered Lord Percy.

Joe waved his empty wallet. "See!"

But he was looking at the swirling snow flakes.

A shape was forming – woolly, white and huge.

The yeti didn't look like a giant hair-ball. It looked like the picture in Lord Percy's notebook. It looked like a walking cloud. In the photo you couldn't see how tall it was. It loomed almost as tall as the tower.

The yeti was looking right at Joe. He could see warm brown eyes through its woolly curls.

All the fear went out of Joe then. He didn't know what was going to happen and suddenly he didn't care.

He started to smile. The world had been magic all this time but Joe had only just found out! He waved at Molly and she waved back, beaming.

The gang leader made a strange gagging sound. He'd seen the yeti. He turned to run but it was too late.

The yeti didn't move. He just breathed out very softly sending a swirl of snowflakes towards the gang.

They started to shrink. They shrank down and down until they looked like little mice in hoodies. Joe heard their tiny voices calling for help.

The yeti blew them lightly into the air with his snowy breath. One by one they landed on his huge hairy hand. The yeti looked across at Joe.

"He wants to know what to do with them," Lord Percy told Joe. "I expect he'll shut them up in a box for a few years if you want."

The gang members were all trying to hide behind each other. Joe felt sorry for them.

"I don't want them shut in a box. I want them to change, like you and McNab," he added in a whisper.

"Tell them, Joe," said Lord Percy.

Joe's voice came out loud and strong. "Stop bullying people and I'll tell the yeti to let you go!"

Lord Percy quickly held up his hand. "Not just yet. Your sister wants to say something!"

Joe was surprised. "What do you want to say, Moll?" he called.

Molly giggled. She looked really pleased with herself.

"Say 'cheese', naughty boys!" she said. **Flash**! His little sister had snapped a picture!

"Plus I've been filming you on Joe's phone! So if you ever bully my brother or anyone

else ever again, this is **definitely** going on YouTube!" she added.

The yeti set the tiny bullies down very softly and slowly. They ran so fast, they were falling over each other in the snow. By the time they reached the gates Joe saw they were almost back to the right size.

Then the yeti bent down to Joe's level and smiled at Lord Percy as if he was saying, "Ready to go home?"

"Yes, we're ready," Lord Percy said softly.

The yeti breathed out another long snowy breath and Lord Percy and McNab went sailing high into the air.

One minute they were there. The next Joe was staring up through swirling snowflakes.

They didn't even say goodbye, he thought.

Then he heard cheerful voices floating down.

"Toodlepip, old beans!"

"Bye, nippers!"

When the snow stopped, Lord Percy, Spoons McNab and the yeti had all gone.

Molly started to cry. "It's not fair! Gramps really wanted to know what happened to Lord Percy and he never even got to meet him!"

"He can read his notebook though," Joe reminded her.

Molly perked up. "I forgot about that. I'll show him when we get home."

Joe took her hand. "Show him after we've been to see Gran."

"OK," she said with a sigh.

That night Joe and Molly sat looking at the yeti movie she'd filmed on Joe's phone. Molly giggled. "I don't know why those bullies were so scared! That yeti was super cute!"

Joe laughed. He laughed because the Countdown Crew was history and because they'd had the best news. Gran was coming home in time for Christmas.

Our books are tested
for children and young people by
children and young people.

Thanks to everyone who consulted on
a manuscript for their time and effort in
helping us to make our books better
for our readers.